The Post-Apocalyptic Adventures Of Van and Gary

Ahh, Real Death!

Chapter 1

With my black and red smock dusted with flour that trailed down onto my marinara-smeared black slacks, I clocked off and started the short drive home. I lit up a cigarette at the first stoplight and found myself unable to take my mind off of the new girl on third shift. Slight as a willow and pale as the moon, the sprite-elf-human hybrid was hard to look away from. Of course, she was only human. Sprites and elves don't exist, unfortunately. But, still, she was pretty.

Bright lights reflected in my rearview mirror, and I realized I was going twenty ticks below the speed limit. The lights were only halogen blue, no red, thankfully. I never have liked dealing with the police. Or rather, being dealt with by the police.

I pressed on the gas pedal for a moment before realizing I was almost at my turn. I flipped on my signal and bid a silent apology to the impatient driver behind me. A minute or so later, I pulled into my parking lot and found an open spot. I grabbed my keys and locked the doors as I stood from my car.

This was a new habit I'd gotten into since my car was stolen a few months earlier by a tweaker. He was caught after taking the police on a high-speed chase that ended two towns away. In spite of my status as the victim, I had to pay 150 dollars to get my car out of the impound lot. Live and learn, I suppose.

Once at the top of my stairs, I fumbled with the key for a bit before finally unlocking the door and stepping in. As soon as I closed the door, a small monster charged me and began clawing at my legs. The monster was my canine companion, Gary. Weighing in at just under 10 pounds and hailing from both Germany and Mexico, my little beast friend always made sure I felt welcome.

I changed out of my filthy clothes, washed my face, took a hit of some weed, and met Gary back at the door. He spun in tight circles as I picked up his collar and leash but stood still for the time it took to hook him up.

Down the stairs and across the parking lot, Gary ran toward my car, hoping for a ride, but I led him to the small, enclosed pet area. Once inside the 50 by 100-foot chain link enclosure, I removed his collar and grabbed a poo bag before taking a seat on one of the green metal benches.

I watched Gary sniff out the stories of other dogs by burying his nose in piss-stained grass for a while. A rather loud truck rumbled up to the stop sign a dozen yards away. The intersection included two dead end streets and so there wasn't a lot of traffic at any hour. But anytime loud trucks thought to disturb the peace, Gary was first on the scene.

He booked it from the far end of the pen. Darkness veiled by darkness, he almost looked like a rabbit darting through the short, dense grass. That is, until he let loose with his bloodthirsty battle cry. That battle cry was a series of frantic barks that anyone could identify as coming from a tiny dog.

The truck turned and growled its way around the bend, unconcerned with Gary's objections. Gary stared after the offender and then decided his work was done. He turned away like nothing had happened but just as quickly stopped again.

Something, likely a cat or a possum, had caught his attention and he was staring behind me, through the fence and up the street. Out of appreciation for the symbiosis between man and dog, I always took interest in whatever he found to be noteworthy. I craned my neck to follow his gaze. Then I blinked.

"What the fuck?"

I said it without really noticing that I was speaking. My stomach and testis had switched places and my heart had leveled-up to vibrate mode. I was suddenly aware of a pulsing heat in my legs, and I stood slowly, still entranced by what I was seeing.

It was a person. I assumed it was a man, but they were still a ways up the road and it was a dark, moonless night. The streetlights gave glimpses though. The figure was sprinting, not running, sprinting. He was a bit heavy, that much was obvious even from afar, but he was fucking hauling ass. And coming down the street, toward the intersection, toward the pet area, toward me.

"Gary?"

My own voice seemed to boom in my ears as it mingled with the increasingly audible clamor of the sprinter's footfalls. I blinked again for the first time since seeing the figure. As my eyes opened, all of the idle chatter that had been bouncing around inside my head fled like water through a sieve. Before anything else could happen, the man – I could see him more clearly now, as well as the dark stains running across clothing and flesh alike – opened his mouth wide. Putting the ruckus of the peace disturbing truck to shame, the sprinter let loose a truly bloodthirsty cry.

"Gary!" I shouted.

I spun, searching for the little guy in the dark. He had moved to stand directly behind me and was huddled against my legs, shaking and whimpering. I snatched him up and looked back toward the man just in time to see him collide with the chest high fence not 20 feet away. I let out a yelp of surprise and jumped back.

"Gahh! What the fuck?"

The man answered my knee-jerk rhetorical question with another, even louder cry. I backed away, wide-eyed and terrified. In the dim light I could see that his clothes were not just stained but ripped and stretched. He looked like he'd just left a meeting with his PCP fight club. With a stiff lunge, the man tossed his upper body over the fence and thudded to the ground inside the pen.

I'm just going to lay this out straight: I shit my pants. I'm not sure if it was right then, before then, or after, but I shit my pants, possibly more than once. Thankfully, shitting my pants multiple times wasn't the only thing I did.

With a scream that drown out any sounds coming from my britches, I tucked Gary to my chest, stepped onto the bench to my left and launched myself over the fence. Unfortunately, both of the benches were meant to be set in cement and were, in fact, not set in cement. So, whenever I jumped, the damn thing fell over and my foot clipped the top of the fence. In full running back form, I did a complete flip and landed on my side with a plop, still clutching Gary like a football.

With the air partially knocked out of me, I scrambled to my feet and stumbled away. The sound of the man struggling with the fence got me to look back just in time to see him flip back out of the pen.

"Fuck you, man!" I shouted before darting toward my car. Then I remembered that I left my keys on my kitchen counter. I ignored the car and ran for my apartment. Bare feet slapped against the pavement behind me as I fled through the grass, bypassing the sidewalk. Another roar split the air as I reached the stairs, sounding right fucking behind me. I took the first 4 steps in one groin-splitting lunge and was on the other side of my locked door two seconds later.

"Jesus fuck shit." I gasped.

The phrase meant nothing, but it came directly from my soul. I leaned against the door, still holding Gary. Somewhere in my panicked mind, I thought that I needed his extra weight to hold the door shut and that without him, I'd be as light as a feather.

The entire complex shook as the wild man clamored up the steps. He was making a breathy sound like you might hear from a mentally challenged person if they were upset. It was a pained and drawn-out low hum that came from deep in his throat.

I peered out through the peep hole just in time to see him reach the top of the stairs. I firmed my body in anticipation, but the stupid bastard just ran on through the breezeway. From the sounds that followed, I was pretty certain that the dipshit had ran directly to the stairs on the other side of the building and promptly hurled himself down them. The sounds were accompanied by booming vibrations that rattled the bottles of vodka on my bar, announcing that he'd fallen pretty fucking hard. I marveled for a few moments as it grew quiet around me.

I scanned the breezeway through my peephole with the attentiveness and diligence of a tweaker on the lamb. My eye nearly touched the door as I searched the small pocket of space that was visible through the hole. Nothing else came into view.

Slowly, I sat Gary down and stepped away from the door. Gary instantly darted to my room and scurried under the bed. My breath came in quiet huffs and, when I lifted my hand to my chest, my heart seemed to be beating faster than my hand was shaking. I pulled a few breaths in through my nose and pushed them out of my mouth before walking into my kitchen to find something to fight with.

I'd like to say that I'm not as big of a dipshit as the one that had just plummeted down a flight of stairs, but that might not be accurate. I get agitated whenever one of my neighbors tries to strike up a conversation with me. Something like this happens? Let's just say I wasn't exactly chill.

After finding nothing more than a few pans and small knives in the kitchen, I decided to keep looking. On my way into the bedroom, I saw my tool box sitting next to the utility closet. Kneeling, I flung it open with a rattle of screws, nails, and washers. Inside, I found what I was looking for.

I seized the foot-and-a-half long, 21-ounce, solid steel hammer by it's rubber grip and was quickly back at the door. Once more, I examined the breezeway through the tiny hole and then held my ear to the door after seeing nothing had changed. I hesitated for a moment and wondered briefly why nobody had come out to investigate the racket. Those thoughts washed away as quickly as they had come as I remembered literally having the shit scared out of me by an asshole. It was bullshit poetry of some sort, I was certain, and that pissed me off even more.

Firming my grip on the hammer in my right hand, I unlocked the door with my left and eased it open. I poked my head out and then slipped through, closing the door silently behind me. Without further hesitation, I walked quickly but quietly to the stairs, expecting to see the man prone and bleeding at the bottom. The stairway was clear and only a smear of blood marked where he had landed.

A spike of cold fear flooded my body, and I almost ran back inside. I couldn't let it go, however. I've always been a curious person, and, at that point, I wasn't entirely sure that I hadn't hallucinated the whole ordeal. After all, nobody else seemed to notice the raucous shit show that had surely just shook them in their beds. And, if we're being completely honest, I ate so much acid during my youth that these letters are waving at me as I type them. It's like they're at a Consonant v. Vowel baseball game… But I digress.

With a glance up at the level above me and one more quick look behind, I started down the stairs. Each step was made of a tough, unfinished wood that only got tougher over the years until they were almost as hard as stone. Moving slowly, I leaned over the rail to check the ground floor. A pair of mountain bikes rested against the wall next to a small barbeque grill but there was nothing out of the ordinary. I continued down.

At the bottom, I stood flush with the wall and craned my neck to peer into the night. The sight of the wild man crawling through the grass mere feet to my right probably would've scared the shit out of me if I hadn't already been there and done that. As it was, I let out a squeaking fart. To my horror, the bastard heard it and jerked his body toward me in a lunge. Thankfully, he was in a rather weak position.

Both of his legs were obviously broken, his right arm appeared to have several elbows, and his left hand flopped around uselessly at the wrist. In spite of his laundry list of injuries, the son of a bitch just kept convulsing his fat ass toward me, coughing up blood and phlegm all the while.

I took a step back and goggled at the tableau in front of me. I stared for a moment that seemed to stretch into eternity. In that moment, I was one hundred percent certain that I was looking at a zombie. I stood there slack-jawed, waiting on the doubt and denial to rise up within me. I examined my emotions and searched for the reaction that would make the most sense. I thought frantically, wondering what the hell I was supposed to think, feel, do. I felt nothing. I thought nothing. I could do nothing.

The fury that I had harbored over being made to feel like prey vanished in the presence of shock like darkness before light. My body, being well-trained in what to do during times of stress, injected a wave of hopelessness and depression into my being. Slowly, I lowered my hands to my sides, turned, and walked back up to my apartment, all the while murmuring, "Nope. Nope."

Chapter 2

Some minutes later, I was standing on my balcony in clean pants with four items clutched in my hands as I stared blankly into the woods in front of me. The first was a cigarette. The second, a glass pipe full of weed. The third was a lighter and the fourth, my phone.

I took a long hit from the pipe, lit my cigarette, took another, longer hit from the pipe, pocketed my lighter, and called the cops. As I waited for someone to answer, I pulled my lighter back out and took another hit from the pipe. A voice sounded through the phone half way through my task. Jumping and nearly dropping everything I was holding, I clutched it all to my chest and quested in the mess for my phone.

Putting it back to my ear I said, "Hello. I'm here. Hello?"

"Yes, sir." came a calm feminine reply, "What is your emergency?"

"I… I don't know." I paused only briefly before continuing. "There needs to be police here. That's for sure. Someone's…"

I trailed off, unsure of what I could say without sounding crazy.

"What is your location, sir?" The woman could have easily been asking if I wanted fries with my meal.

I stammered, "Uhh I... err. Fuck." I took a deep breath. "Fox Lane and Grant Street."

"Okay, sir, I'm sending a squad car over now. Is anybody injured?"

I nodded.

"Sir?"

"Yes." I said, realizing she couldn't see my nod, "Somebody's injured."

"How are they injured, sir?"

"Broken bones, blood everywhere."

This time, there was a pause before the operator responded. "Can you tell me what happened?"

No "sir" that time, I noticed. I had started the call by dropping the phone and then proceeded to stammer my way through the first half of the conversation. But my voice had turned cold and certain when she asked about the injured. When I next spoke, my voice was grave.

"I don't think that I can." I said. "Not right now. Send more than one car."

With that, I raised my cigarette to my lips and lowered the phone from my ear, ending the call.

I remained on the balcony for a few minutes, watching the night sky as I finished smoking my bowl. I tapped it out on my palm and tossed the ash into the wind. A few deep breaths later, I picked up the hammer and made my way back outside and down the stairs just in time to watch the cops pull up.

The second car arrived moments after the first. Both had their lights going but no sirens.

There was no need so close to midnight in such a small town. I rounded the building and came into view on the end opposite the zombie man.

The officers quickly exited their vehicles and drew their sidearms, pointing them at my chest as they shouted instructions. I froze with one foot in the air and raised my hands over my head. I dropped the hammer and it clattered to the ground.

"Now, get on the ground!" Both officers were yelling, "Do it now!"

I dropped to my knees on the pavement but decided that it was a bad time to remain silent.

"I'm the one who called." I said, keeping my hands in the air, "You know me, I think. I work at the pizza shop. I do the deliveries."

The officers stopped shouting but continued to close the distance between us. I really didn't want to be pressed to the ground and handcuffed out there. What if another zombie showed up?

"I didn't hurt anybody." I continued, hoping my reputation as an inconsequential and lonely bachelor would come to my defense.

"Look at the hammer. It's clean. I only have it out because someone attacked me."

They finally stopped their advance. Standing about 10 feet away, they looked me over and then shared a look with each other. I kept my head low but noticed the air of uncertainty that passed between the two. The first officer on the scene turned his head, met my eyes, and asked a simple question.

"What happened?"

I drew in a long and weary breath and then released it in a huff before stammering my way through the night's events. Whether I should have or not, I even told them about searching the man out once I retrieved a weapon. After I told them about what I had found at the bottom of the stairs, however, they didn't seem very interested in my intent to exact retribution. One of the officers grabbed the hammer and the other helped me to my feet.

"Show us where he is."

The officer that spoke was a tall, husky guy with a long face. I recognized the pizza fan without needing to read his badge. His name was Sean or Officer Sean Taylor, depending on the situation. I led him and the other officer, a portly fellow named Dan, around the corner and to the foot of the stairs that the zombie man had fallen down.

"Where is he?" Officer Dan asked. "If he's as badly injured as you said then he didn't just walk away."

I opened my mouth to answer when a choking cough broke the quiet of the night. Both officers spun toward the sound, their hands going to the guns on their hips. When they saw what had made the sound, they shared my earlier sentiments, almost in unison.

"What the fuck?"
"What the fuck?"

The zombie man had crawled about 20 feet away and was laying in the middle of the grassy lawn. Blood still ran from his mouth and down his chin. In his attempt to lurch back toward the building, he'd also bent himself awkwardly at the waist. His face was a rictus of pain and rage as he clawed at the ground with both hands, including the broken one, which only ground into the dirt, removing flesh with each pass. Another wet cough left his mouth and dark fluid sprayed through the air with it. Both officers backed toward the building, leaving me out front.

“What the fuck?” Officer Dan repeated, deciding to take his gun out after all.

“What did you do to him?” Sean asked.

I threw my arms out to the side as if I were an athlete challenging a call by the referee.

“I told you what happened.” I said then gestured toward the monster in the grass. “How could I even do that to somebody?”

Dan’s eyes stayed glued to the zombie man. Sean’s gaze shifted back and forth from it to me. Finally, he stepped forward, probably feeling like a douche after putting me between himself and the danger. Dan stayed where he was. He might even have taken another step back.

“You don’t know how this happened?” Sean asked.

I cocked my head. “You mean how a zombie ended up chasing me and my dog around like a cat after a fucking mouse?” I shook my head. “No. Can’t say that I do. Can’t say that I know the fucker’s origin story, officer.”

The strained look in his eyes said that he didn’t appreciate my tone. I’d normally have been more cautious with the police but after running for my life from a mad man that turned out to be some sort of undead monster, I was feeling like a bit of a wild card.

“Sorry.” I said, “But no. I don’t know what is happening. I was going to fight the fucking guy when I thought he was just a drunk on PCP.”

“Maybe that’s it.” Sean said, sounding hopeful. “Maybe he’s just on something.”

I raised an eyebrow but didn’t say anything. He clearly needed something to believe other than ‘it’s the zombie apocalypse’. Dan seemed to be comforted by the notion as well.

“Yeah.” He said, taking a step forward and nodding. Though his eyes didn’t leave the zombie. “Those bath salts can really mess a guy up. He needs help.”

As if on queue, an ambulance rounded the corner and pulled in behind the squad cars. I got Sean’s attention and gestured toward my pocket. Then I made a peace sign and held it to my lips.

He waved dismissively and moved to intercept the techs. I followed, not wanting to be left alone with Officer Freaked, and reached into my pocket for a cigarette. The zombie man was still writhing in the grass, his frantic efforts to pursue everybody at once making him into even more of a lurching, seizing mess.

I heard a sliding glass door slam open above and turned back in time to see a form descend from a third-story balcony. I had just enough time to recognize the form as a neighbor that I had pegged as a violent alcoholic before the man crashed to the ground, taking Officer Dan with him. Bones cracked as the two hit the pavement and Dan's panicked screams were mixed with the same low hum of the moronic as I had heard before.

"Fucking shoot, it!" I shouted. Never mind that I was commanding the police to shoot a civilian. I knew what needed to be done.

Sean unholstered his gun and aimed at the man attacking his fellow officer.

"Stand down!" He shouted, "Sir!"

Dan suddenly pulled his knee in and kicked his assailant free. In the moments before it was on him again, he rolled over to where his gun had fallen and snatched it up. Just as Sean was moving in, Dan raised his gun and put a round into his attacker's chest.

I had been stepping back since the beginning of the attack, but the crack of the gunshot froze me. I stared at the smoking hole in the man's upper breast and then shifted my gaze to Dan. Then on to Sean and the techs. Everyone stood motionless, as if in a trance. I turned back to face Dan and saw what had caught their attention. It was something I hadn't noticed at first in the dimly lit commotion. Dan was not in good shape.

Even as my eyes focused on him, he threw his head back and began to groan. The groan quickly turned into a pained growl. His head snapped forward and his rapid breathing made him sound like Forrest Gump imitating his mother in bed with his school principal.

Bare seconds passed before one of the techs moved in to tend to the fallen officer. The other quickly shook free of her shock and rushed to the figure groaning on the lawn. I saw what was about to happen and stepped in to cut off the tech that was closing in on Dan.

"Stop!" I shouted at him.

His jogging step faltered, and he turned to face me. Behind him, I could see the female tech trying to approach the zombie man. I barreled past Sean and the bemused tech shouting seemingly unrelated phrases.

"He's already gone! Don't! Fuck, I don't have it!"

The woman stopped and looked up as I began shouting. When I was 10 feet away, the zombie man finally succeeded in grabbing the tech's leg. She screamed and fell with a muted thud. I reached them a breath later and brought my heel down across the monster's head. I was wearing sneakers, but I had built up some momentum with my dash across the lawn. Additionally, my foot landed just beneath the bastard's right ear. The result was a bad case of broken neck. Zombie guy finally lay still, save for the twitching.

A gunshot behind me made me turn so fast that I slipped and fell on the damp lawn. I reoriented myself and looked toward Sean and the tech. Turns out, pretty much the exact same thing that happened with me and lady tech also happened with Sean and sir tech. The only difference was that Sean had a gun.

While I was charging at zombie man, the tech decided he would treat whoever needed treatment and that was that. Harrumph! So, he got close enough to Officer Dan for him to reach out and grab the poor fool. Sean wasn't fucking around though. He had been catching onto the vibe for a minute and wasn't taking any chances. He already had his gun drawn and aimed before Dan had even lifted his arm toward the tech. A spray of blood and brains on the sidewalk said that Officer Dan would never rise again.

By the time I lifted myself from the wet grass and found myself in a position to see what was happening, I heard another glass door slide open. My heart lurched at the thought of an addition to this mad-house rendition of Night of the Living Dead. But when I looked up, it was just a concerned looking older woman huddling in her pink robe. I remembered seeing her often. She had a miniature poodle and a fat wiener dog that always barked at me.

"What's going on?" She called down to us. "Is everything okay?"

I was relieved that she wasn't a zombie. I was also confused as shit as to why she hadn't come out sooner. We were not being quiet out there. Still, it took 2 gunshots for her to take notice and she was the only fucking one who did! It was becoming increasingly clear to me that this was all just a hallucination.

“Ma’am…” Officer Sean began but I interrupted.

“No.” I said, “Everything is fucked up. Stay inside and start prepping for a disaster.”

When she didn’t move, I shouted, “Go!”

The woman straightened but made no move to close her door.

“Fine.” I said, resignedly, “Stay out here with the fucking zombies. I think we’ve gathered 3 dead bodies down here over the past 90 seconds. Care to come help for a minute?”

For the first time, the woman looked to her left and saw the 2 dead beneath the adjacent balcony.

“Oh my god!” She gasped and then accused, “What did you do?”

“There’s no fucking way you’re talking to me!” I shouted up and took several steps toward her.

“Hey!” Officer Sean bellowed.

I realized then that he had been attempting to take back control of the situation ever since I had yanked it away. All eyes fell on the remaining officer. Everyone waited for the guy with a gun to speak.

"Ma'am," he said, looking up to meet her eyes, "Please stay inside and lock your doors. I don't know what is happening, but you do not want to be out here right now."

The woman hesitated, clearly about to boil over with questions and accusations. After a moment however, she slipped back inside, latching the door behind her and drawing the curtains closed. Sean turned his gaze on me, and I had the good grace to look abashed. His approach was inarguably more effective than mine was.

The male tech was still standing next to the body of the fallen officer, shock plastered across his face. He glanced at Sean and then at his partner who was absently brushing her pants off while staring open mouthed at the zombie man. His eyes moved back to the dead officer. Correction, the murdered officer.

"Why did you do that?" He asked and then louder, "What is wrong with you?"

"You don't understand." I began, "These guys aren't just sick…"

“Look out!”

The shout had come from the lady tech. I spun and saw a figure just as it swung around the corner and barreled toward us. Before Sean could raise his weapon, he was tackled to the ground, his gun tumbling away through the grass.

“Holy shit!” I screeched, “Ahh!”

Screeching or not, I didn’t just stand there. With a few quick steps I snatched Officer Dan’s sidearm up off the sidewalk and spun back to face the fucker. I was too late.

The newest zombie was straddling Sean’s chest and her thumbs had quickly found the officer’s eyes. Dark red blood flowed out around the creature’s hands. They were dug in so deeply that her wrists were nearly inside the officer’s skull too. With a series of sharp yanks, the neck broke, and Sean’s body lay still. It was over in just a few seconds.

I raised the gun in both hands and squeezed the trigger twice. One bullet entered the shoulder and the other went in through the left cheek. Blood and teeth spewed into the air and the aggressor fell to the ground… for a moment.

No sooner than her body hit the ground, she was springing back to her feet and gurgling a roar as she threw herself at me. Two more rounds left the gun that was clutched in my hands. One entered the same cheek I'd hit before. More teeth flew into the air. The other hit the center of her throat. The bitch dropped, spasming violently. From the direction of the ambulance, footfalls and snarls marked the coming of more.

I turned and shouted, "Come with me!"

Even as I opened my mouth to shout, another figure burst from the shadows of some trees and bore the female tech to the ground with a sickening crunch. The male tech ran toward her shouting, "Sara!" but I knew it was too late. The others were nearly upon us, and more were probably on their way. Even as I had the thought, I heard glass shattering and people screaming in the other apartment buildings up the street.

I yelled after the man, "You can't help her!" He probably didn't even hear me.

I fired at the approaching zombies but didn't hit anywhere that slowed them down. The fastest of the creatures was on the unnamed tech in an instant and quickly had the man's throat in one hand and his jaw in the other. It reached into his mouth and was trying to wrench the poor man's face in two. I fired another useless shot, cursed, and spun to get away.

In the process of running away, my foot hit something in the grass. Without looking down, I stooped and grabbed the other gun before bolting up the stairs and into my apartment.

Unlike the first time, I had to brace my door against the onslaught of assailants. As soon as the deadbolt clicked into place, they hit. I leaned against my door, covered in sweat that was more from stress than exertion, and wondered if they would've passed by had I not engaged the lock.

I huddled there, grateful that I at least hadn't shit my pants again, and cried at the death that was surrounding me. I cried for the murdered and the murderers alike. I cried for Gary and myself. I wept for the future.

Chapter 3

Several minutes passed and each of them felt like hours. The attacking mass was relentless. I wanted to know how many there were, but I refused to do anything but press my body against the door as I sobbed gently.

A voice sounded amid the moans and bangs saying, “Hey! Hey, what are you doing?”

Suddenly, the banging stopped. I stayed where I was, listening and waiting. In the unnatural silence that followed, I heard the same gruffly feminine voice again. It was quieter this time.

"What the fuck?"

The question was immediately followed by the thunderous sound of zombies falling over one another and down the stairs. Whoever the brave woman was, she ran away shrieking, her screams gradually fading until she was out of earshot.

I waited, tense, for the bastards to come back. Long seconds passed with nothing happening. Sweat and tears trickled down my face before being absorbed into my damp shirt. I lifted my head to peer through the peephole once more. The breezeway was clear.

Stifling an audible sigh of relief, I slid to the floor and buried my face in my hands. It was then that I realized I was still holding the officers' guns. I whacked myself in the face with one before I could stop myself. It didn't go off, praise Allah, but it hurt like a fuck. Momentarily unconcerned with remaining quiet, I hurled the firearms across the room and into the wall.

Neither weapon discharged upon impact, nor as they tumbled to rest on the carpeted floor. But seconds after, a steady thumping vibrated the floor beneath my ass. It was an unmistakable message and I received it instantly. My neighbors wanted me to keep it down.

"Are you fucking kidding me?" I bellowed.

Three more rhythmic thumps rang out through the floor, traveling directly from their fists and into my rectum. I fucking lost it. Between my initial terror at being pursued and the deaths that had recently taken place around me, I was ready to go to war with the next fly that so much as buzzed near me.

With a snarl that almost matched the zombies, I pushed myself to my feet. Without a single thought beyond finally confronting my shitty downstairs neighbor, I flung the door open and stepped outside. Although, even in my state of mindless fury, I spared a moment to close the door so Gary wouldn't get out. That is, if he ever came out from under the bed again.

I got to the top of the stairs closest to my front door and froze. A mass of tangled bodies writhed at the bottom. It looked like 3 were caught between crawling free of the mess and snapping at their peers for getting in the way. One more lay motionless and I wasn't sure if it was a dead zombie or just a regular dead guy. Either way, he was pretty fucking dead.

The sight of the zombies brought me back to my senses for the most part and I ran back inside, still pissed off at the whole shitty situation. I picked up the discarded handguns and made my way to the balcony. I leaned out over the rail in order to get a better view of the zombies but hesitated. I pulled myself back and shook my head. After lighting up a cigarette, I sat one of the guns down and leaned back out over the railing.

With my left hand gripping the doorframe of the balcony storage room, I sighted with the gun in my right and pulled the trigger. Six yards away, a head snapped back, and fluids splattered the wall. I sighted again, having more trouble lining up a shot after further agitating the beasts.

Sure or no, I took a shot and struck another one. The bullet only hit the chest, but the force of the shot knocked the fucker back and its head split open on a hard wood step. The third and final thorn in my side was finally free from thc pile but still on the ground. No amount of elbow room could change the fact that its legs dragged uselessly behind it.

Unperturbed, I took careful aim and pulled the trigger. It was another shower of teeth and blood as my shot was lower than I wanted. The bullet must have hit something important though because the bastard finally lay down, only moving in convulsions.

I pulled myself back onto the balcony and slipped inside, for once unconcerned with the 'no smoking' policy. Moving into the kitchen, I flipped on the light and ejected the clips from each gun, emptied them, and added up my supply.

I had one full clip and three rounds to spare. Nodding to myself, I reloaded the magazines and stuffed the one with fewer shots into my waistband. On second thought, I pulled the gun out of my waistband, engaged the safety, and then replaced it. As I turned to leave the kitchen, I saw through the open doorway to my bedroom noticed a little black nose sticking out from underneath my bed.

"Hey, buddy." I said, stooping to the floor and sitting my gun to the side.

"It's okay, buddy." I said soothingly.

He poked his head out an inch or two to get a look at my face. With a small whimper, he looked away and scooted back under the bed. I sighed and picked up the gun. Back on my feet, I started to leave but hesitated. I went to the kitchen and filled a few of my biggest pans with water and sat them on the floor. I also opened Gary's bag of food and lay it on its side before kneeling next to my bed once more.

"I'll be back, buddy."

I stood and moved to the door. Seeing nothing through the hole, I took a deep breath and was soon outside again. The air seemed warmer, but I knew that it was my own blood making me hot. I took a few more deep breaths and started down the stairs at the far end of the breezeway.

Again, I searched from the stairs for anything below. Again, I saw nothing and reached the bottom a few steps later. The night was as still as the grave and twice as eerie. The quiet was almost deafening in its contrast to the gunshots and screaming earlier.

Around the corner, I could see the two squad cars and the single ambulance, lights still flashing on all of them. With a few paranoid glances, I took off in a crouch with my gun held out in front of me in both hands. I swept from side to side like I'd seen done in movies, but I saw nothing. I approached Sean's car carefully, still looking over my shoulders more than I was watching where I was going. I jumped through the open door into the driver's seat and pulled the door shut behind me.

Inside, I emptied the glove box and was delighted to find two more full clips. I pulled the gun out of my waistband and replaced the clip with a new one. Grinning slightly, I sat both guns in the seat next to me and started rummaging through the center console.

"Umm. Hey…"

The voice was soft, but it came from right next to my ear.

"Ahhhhhhh!" I cried out like a little girl and pawed desperately at the guns and the door handle at the same time.

"No!" Came the voice again. "Please don't shoot me!"

I stopped flailing and turned my head to look in the back. The metal and glass that separated the front from the back made it difficult to make out details in the dark, but I thought I knew who it was.

"Van?" Came the small voice.

I froze, now certain that I knew who it was.

"Van?" She repeated and leaned forward, squinting.

I faced forward and pitched my voice low to disguise it.

"I don't have a van." I said, "Wouldn't just give it away if I did."

The woman in the back sighed deeply. "Oh my god, Van. Shut the fuck up and get me out of here. What's happening? Where are the cops?"

I sighed as well and turned to face her. "What are you doing here, Gwyn?"

My voice was flat and resigned. Gwyn and I had dated off and on as teenagers. It was really just a series of short-lived and volatile endeavors that were centered around our mutual desires to fuck one another. It ended for good on a drunken night that tends to float just out of range of my recollection. Whether that's because of the liquor or the shame, or both, I can't be sure. I didn't ever hit her or hurt her physically. But there are other ways to mistreat a person.

“Uhmm…” She began, already sounding bitchy, “I’m pretty sure I have more of a right to be in here than you do.”

I met her eyes for a moment longer before looking away with a muttered curse. She had me there. She was probably given a personal invitation and everything. My eyes fell on the guns in the passenger seat.

“You don’t know what’s happened.” I said, still not meeting her eyes. “There are at least ten dead bodies over there.”

Her eyes widened. “What!”

“Shhhh!” I held my hands up and glanced out through the windows.

“Seriously?” She said, cocking her head, “You screamed like a bitch just a minute ago. That was way louder than I was.”

I gritted my teeth and closed my eyes. I took several deep breaths before opening them. Finally meeting her eyes through the cage, I continued.

“I didn’t mean to scream. But you’re right, we shouldn’t do that. There are fucking monsters in the night that want to kill everyone.”

I paused, waving my hand in front of my face and then pointing at my eyes.

"Look at me," I said, "I have personally killed five people tonight."

In spite of my efforts to be taken seriously, Gwyn let out a mocking laugh. I looked away from her and fingered one of guns. Her laughter cut off.

"Van, don't fuck with me." She suddenly sounded serious. "I heard the gunshots and screams."

She paused to work some moisture into her mouth and then asked that wonderful question. The question I always love to answer. The one that brings up such cherished memories.

"What happened?"

I sighed again but figured it'd be best to start at the beginning. A couple of minutes later, Gwyn sat back hard enough to rock the car a bit, a look of disbelieving horror on her pale face. I finished my story with me deciding to look for more ammo and weapons in the cars, where I found her.

"I found you." She said offhandedly, as if she didn't know she was speaking. "You didn't even know I was here."

I countered, "Even when treasure sings, the one who uncovers it is still the one who found it."

She lifted an eyebrow, "So I'm treasure, am I?"

I opened my mouth to reply but then snapped it shut. I knew better than to fall into her traps. I was ready. Oh yes. I was ready.

Seeing that she wasn't going to get a response she spoke again. This time her tone was more subdued.

"So, they're all dead?"

I gave a solemn nod and let my gaze fall to my hands again. I could feel her eyes on me. The weight of them pressed against me and I lifted my head to meet her eyes. She was crying.

"Gwyn?"

"I'm so sorry, Van." Her words came out as a whisper, and she buried her face in her hands. "You always hated violence. I'm sorry."

My throat tightened at seeing her tears. I found my own eyes damp after her reminder that we once knew each other. I glanced toward my apartment and then into the world of blue and red on either side of the car. I reached for the handle just as a body slammed into my door. I reeled back and barked my surprise, managing to abstain from any undignified screaming for once.

Gwyn did not join me in the practice. An earsplitting scream burst from her like a wind demon. I grunted in pain and threw my arms over my ears.

"Gwyn!" I shouted again, "Gwyn!" Finally, I yelled, "Shut the fuck up, Gwyneth!"

That got her to stop. She stared at me with wide eyes and then back at the creature beating against the window. Before she could start up again, I covered my left ear with my hand and pressed my other ear into my shoulder as I took aim at the beast.

"Cover your ears!"

It was moving around too much for me to line up a head shot, and I didn't want the thing jumping through the weakened glass after I fired. So, I placed three rounds in its chest in the space of a second. That did the trick, but Gwyn screamed again.

"Gwyn!" I shouted, then continued in a calm, if strained, voice. "I'm going to come let you out. You can't scream. I need you to follow me very closely. Don't run unless I tell you to and keep your eyes and your ears open. Do you understand?"

She nodded, surprising me by doing so. I expected… Something else. I'd never known her to take well to being told what to do. A paranoid part of me thought she was going to wait until I let her out and then slap me in the face. Or worse, in the dick.

I ignored that part of my brain and opened the door. There didn't appear to be any more zombies nearby, so I helped Gwyn out and reached back into the car to grab the keys.

I urged her to hunch over and move quickly toward the ambulance. There was an enraged roar somewhere up the street and it made Gwyn jump and let out a little squeak. At least her squeak came from her mouth. I was really not looking forward to shitting my pants in front of her.

With my hand pressed into her back, we quickly reached the large doors of the ambulance and were soon inside. She moved to the back of the cab as I tied the doors shut with a strap from the table. I picked my gun back up and took a few steps toward her.

She tensed for a moment before closing the distance between us and throwing her arms around me in a big sloppy hug. She followed it up with an equally sloppy kiss. I pulled back, surprised, but she just leaned in further and kissed me again. I didn't pull away the second time. I wrapped my arms around her and leaned into her embrace, appreciating the gentleness of the moment.

We eventually separated and sat down on the bench next to the gurney. My mind was racing in circles, and I couldn't think of anything worth saying. That wasn't an issue for very long. With a quick motion, Gwyn slapped me across the face just hard enough for it to sting. I suppressed a cry of protest and instead settled with an indignant glare.

She said as casually as if she had just placed money in my hand for the valet. "That's for telling me to shut the fuck up and for using my full name."

I stared at her incredulously. Between the zombies and her kissing me, it took me a moment to even remember what she was talking about. When I finally did remember, I started to laugh. It began as a chuckle and quickly turned into wheezing heaves that shook my frame. Gwyn swatted my arm and told me to be quiet, but I couldn't help myself. It was too much.

In the space of an hour, I had been pursued by zombies, watched four people be murdered, and killed six other people. Not to mention all of the crying and shitting my pants. Then, I ran into one of my exes in the process of looting a cop car and, to top it all off, she seemed to want to get back together as much as she wanted to kick my ass. It was easily one of the top 13 weirdest nights of my life.

With an exertion of will, I steadied my breathing and wiped the tears from my eyes. Gwyn was staring at me with her mouth open, shaking her head slowly. I rested my hand on hers and took another deep breath before speaking.

"I'm sorry." I chuckled again but cut it short. "It's been a long night. I think it's finally catching up with me."

She gave me an understanding nod. “It’ll be okay, Van. We’ll figure this out.”

I looked up from where I had rested my hand atop hers and smiled. She tilted her almond shaped face to the side, her long black hair streaming over her shoulders, and favored me with a demure grin in return. I stared into her dark eyes and remembered her from a decade earlier. She was not so beautiful then. Gorgeous, sure. But nothing like she was in the back of that ambulance. Never more beautiful.

Somewhere deep in my mind, I knew that my emotions were running high and that I couldn’t trust any decisions based on them. Closer to the surface, I knew that I had been scared and alone before I found her, and I didn’t want her to go. That thought reminded me of something else.

“Gary is still in my apartment.”

“You still have Gary?”

I scrunched my face up. “Of course, I still have Gary. Why wouldn’t I?”

She shrugged. “It’s just been a long time. I remember when you first got him.”

I nodded, also remembering. Her little sister had gotten Gary as a puppy but didn't show any interest in actually caring for him. None of her family did either. One day, I was tripping on acid when I went to visit Gwyn and I saw the little guy covered in flees and so malnourished that his hair had almost completely fallen out. The sight wrenched at my acid steeped soul, and I immediately left to get medicine for him. Whenever I returned to give them the meds, they asked if I wanted to just take him home with me. I eagerly accepted the offer, and he was back to full health in less than a month.

"Yeah," I said, "It's been a while." I shook myself free of the memory and continued, "He's all alone up there right now. I was thinking we could grab him and whatever else we can find in the cop cars and take off in this ambulance."

"Shouldn't we wait on more cops?" She asked as if it were obvious and then added, "This isn't a video game."

"I don't think this can be solved by a few more cops." I said, "Listen."

We fell still and silent, listening. Through the walls of the cabin, the sounds of scattered screams drifted in. A faint gunshot could be heard, then nothing for a few heartbeats, then more screams.

"This might not be a video game." I said, "But it's not looking a lot like real life either. Those are fucking zombies, or I didn't shit my pants twice tonight."

There was a moment of silence and I wished that somebody would scream or fire off a shot. Nobody did. I considered firing my own gun.

"You shit your pants?" She put her hand over her nose and mouth as if she could smell it, but I knew she was hiding a smile. "That's fucking gross."

My face reddened and my jaw clenched. "I changed my clothes, Gwyn. And even if I didn't, I earned those shitty britches. I won't be shamed."

My final statement was only slightly undercut by my beet-red face. Gwyn lowered her hand from her face and revealed a broad, sympathetic grin. I started to feel a bit better. Then she spoke.

"I like your plan." She paused. "Though, I guess we'll have to stop somewhere and pick up some diapers for you, huh?"

My face split into a toothy grin and I laughed. "I will not be shamed, woman. After the night I've had, I may very well start wearing diapers again."

She laughed and quickly covered her smile with her hand. That was a habit I doubted she would ever outgrow. Her teeth were not perfect, but nor were they in any way unseemly. The flaw was in her self image, not her incisors.

"Do you know how to use a gun?" I asked.

She stopped laughing and looked down at my hand. "You want me to have the gun? Why?"

I shook my head. "Not "the" gun."

I pulled the other gun out of my waistband and proffered it. Reluctantly, she took the weapon, showing enough presence of mind to not point it at either of us. She quickly ejected the clip and counted the rounds. Before she could ask, I handed over one of the full clips from Sean's car. She loaded the magazine, chambered a round, and flipped the safety off.

More than slightly aroused, I untied the straps on the doors and eased them open. Not hearing any screaming nearby, I stepped out and spun in a quick circle, listening intently. Gwyn followed close behind, her thin arms somehow keeping the gun aloft. I moved to the car that I'd yet to pilfer and checked the glove box and center console before moving on to the trunk.

Inside, I found a duffle bag, a bullet proof vest, a first aid kit, and a shotgun. With Gwyn covering me, I grabbed every bit of it. The bag was heavy, but I didn't complain. Heavy meant full. I threw the vest over my head and tucked the rest under my arm. My ears pricked up as they caught the faint sound of snarling behind me.

"It's by the stop sign." Gwyn whispered, almost too soft for me to hear, "It doesn't see us."

I swallowed hard and turned slowly, crouching as low as I could without falling on my ass. Suddenly, Gwyn yanked me up and pushed me toward my building. At first, I thought she was using me as bait. Then I thought she was using me as a distraction so she could get away. Then I realized what she had been shouting at me.

"…sees us! He sees us!"

Without asking for further clarification, I joined her in sprinting toward my apartment.

"My keys are in my pocket!" I yelled.

"Get them out!"

"My hands are full!" I shot back.

She growled, startling me even in my panic, turned and fired. I hadn't realized how close the zombie had gotten. By the time the first bullet hit, it was less than 20 feet away. The first two shots hit high but the last two hit just right of center. It went down in a heap.

Without a word, she spun back to face me and quested roughly in my pocket before yanking out my keys as well as the fabric of my pocket. I yelped at being jerked up by my pants. She seemed a bit chagrinned but otherwise unrepentant as she held the keys up in front of me. I gestured at the one that would unlock my door and led her up the stairs.

Chapter 4

We ended up not leaving with the ambulance. After our short but intense journey inside, neither of us was eager to go back out. Instead, we took turns getting cleaned up in the bathroom and slowly coaxed Gary out from under the bed.

While Gwyn was in the shower, I took a moment to shove all of my furniture up against the door. I worried about the balcony door for a moment but put it out of my mind. The zombies could barely handle stairs. I doubted they would think to scale the side of the building. Still, I flipped the latch down.

Gwyn came out of the bathroom wearing a pair of my jeans and one of my shirts. The jeans were rolled up her legs until they resembled long shorts. The shirt was a stretchy one that I used to exercise in. The black fabric hugged her lithe form tightly and I had to turn away in order to keep from gawking.

After my own stint in the shower, I changed into some clean clothes for the second time that night and rejoined Gwyn in the living room. The sight of her sitting in my recliner, watching South Park on Comedy Central with Gary in her lap caught me completely off guard. I froze on the edge of the room and Gwyn turned to face me.

"What?" She asked.

"This is just weird." I said. "It's sort of surreal to see you here. Even considering…" I waved my arm at the door, "everything else that's happened."

She nodded solemnly, as if she could relate to what I was feeling. She'd known me for nearly a decade whenever we parted ways and so I figured she did understand. I wasn't a very social person and never had been. As I said, my dog was my best friend. What I didn't say is that he was kind of my only friend, not counting the two coworkers that I got along with. When it came to having friends over, I didn't. As far as girlfriends, spouses and families went, I had none and no interest in finding a way to get them.

My closest family lived about one hundred miles away. They owned land down there and had lived peacefully upon it for more than a couple of generations. They farmed cattle as well as hay and made more than a decent living doing it. And I wanted nothing to do with them.

It wasn't anything personal. Or, well, I suppose it was as personal as personal gets. Though, I didn't see it that way. I just wanted to be my own man. I wanted even to shed the burden of such a moniker and be my own person. It didn't turn out to be as glamorous as I had hoped it would. But I wasn't complaining… very often.

"It's been a weird night." Gwyn said, interrupting my thoughts.

"It has," I agreed and then smiled, "Want to make it freaky?"

I punctuated the question with a waggle of my eyebrows. Gwyn laughed and her hand shot up to cover her mouth again. I rolled my eyes internally at her apparent notion that insecurity was less unbecoming than a genuine smile and moved to sit on the couch. Gary jumped out of her lap and into mine, settling back down instantly.

"Did you go through the stuff?" I asked, rubbing behind Gary's ears.

She shook her head. "I waited for you."

I adopted a dreamy expression, clasping my hands under my chin.

"For me?" I asked, blinking wildly in an attempt to bat my eyelashes.

It was her turn to roll her eyes, though, she didn't hide her exasperation. I chuckled and moved Gary aside. He was used to my fidgety nature and so he didn't complain. I gathered the duffle bag, shotgun, first aid kit, and the few other things I could snatch up and laid them out across the floor. Upon further consideration, I lay both handguns next to the arrangement. Seeing it all laid out that way gave me a sense of security that I had sorely been missing.

“What do you think is in the bag?” Gwyn asked.

“I don’t know.” I said, “I haven’t really thought about it. I was just hoping to find some shotgun shells in there.”

“Well, open it.” She said, sounding eager, “Let’s see.”

“Hang on.”

I leaned forward onto all fours and crawled behind the recliner.

“What the fuck are you doing?”

She tried to sound mildly scathing but her tone betrayed her uneasiness at seeing me crawling around. Within the surreal normality of my living room, it was easy to forget the horrors in the night. I stood on my knees and reached out, resting my hand on her arm.

“I’m just grabbing something.” I squeezed gently and then bent back down.

I crawled backward to my spot on the floor with a small tin canister in hand. It was the kind you might use to gift cookies. I removed the lid and pulled out a bag of weed along with my pipe and grinder. I left behind the papers, not feeling up for a joint. A few minutes later, we were passing the pipe back and forth as I emptied the duffle.

I was pleased to find a full case of shotgun shells as well as a small tent, several road flares, and a package of emergency rations. There was also an ammunition strap tucked inside. What really caught my eye though was the hand grenade.

"Holy shit." Gwyn said as I lifted it out of the bag. "Is that real?"

I shook my head and stared intently at the small object. "It feels real." I rotated it in my hand and shook my head again. "What was a cop doing with this fucking thing?"

"I don't know," Gwyn said, shifting uneasily in her seat, "But put it away."

I stood carefully and scanned my apartment for a safe place to store a grenade. After seeing no good options, I lowered my standards and scanned again. In the end, I sat it in the produce drawer of my fridge and called it good.

Back in the living room, I handed Gwyn the tin can and asked her to load another bowl. As she did, I looked through the first aid kit. It wasn't a full surgical kit, but then, I didn't know how to perform surgery. It was nice though, for a first aid kit. It even had a shot of Naloxone, the drug used to counteract opioid overdoses, along with needle and thread, disinfectant, and an array of different bandages and salves.

"What are we going to do?"

The question was yet another simple one but, again, I was thrown off by it. I had been intentionally avoiding thoughts of what to do beyond checking the loot. I felt an irrational urge to suggest we never leave my apartment. But I knew we wouldn't last long.

"I don't know." I shrugged and said, "I tried calling the cops but that didn't really work out."

"Can we stay here?" She asked.

"For now." I said, unsure if I should tell her the rest. I sighed, deciding she needed to know. "I don't have much food here. There are some rations, but they won't last us more than a week or so. Assuming this building remains standing, and the door isn't kicked in, we'll be okay in here until then. After that, we'll have to figure something else out."

Realization spread across her face as I spoke. Until then, she had been maintaining some measure of an illusion that the craziness of the night was just that and that everything would go back to normal by the time the sun rose. Now considering the possibility of staying inside until hunger forced us out, her face grew pale, and she stood. Without preamble, she grabbed the couch and started pulling it away from the door.

"What are you doing?" I asked, jumping up in alarm.

"I can't stay here." She said as she wrestled with the furniture. "I can't just stay here. I have things I have to do. I have to go. I can't stay here."

She spoke faster and faster with each short sentence, not seeming to realize that she was rambling. I stepped close to her and placed a hand on her shoulder. She spun and pushed me away. I was so caught off guard that her slight push sent me stumbling away and I had to grab the wall to keep from falling.

Gritting my teeth and suddenly remembering why we went our separate ways; I stepped up behind her and wrapped one arm around her waist. The other reached her mouth just as she started to scream at me to put her down and let her go. Yes, I remembered all too well my past struggles to reason with the woman. I decided without actually deciding anything that I wasn't going to fight with her. I decided that she was going to listen to me and accept what I had to say for once in her goddamn life. I carried her back to the recliner and plopped her down in it.

"Listen to me." I began. It came out as a harsh whisper though I did not intend it to. "There are monsters out there. You will die if you go running into the night like a fucking idiot. Think, Gwyn. Hey."

The last word was accompanied by my outstretched hand reaching up to palm her jaw. I made her look at me, and her eyes widened at the look on my face. I'd been a fairly chill guy for most of my adult life. My father, however, was a severe man and he often wore severe expressions. My parentage shone through in that moment.

"Listen to me." I continued with more force, tightening my grip on her jaw. "If you run out there and die, I'll be stuck here dealing with my own depression until the food runs out. Now take some deep breaths and stop acting like a trapped fucking rat."

I yanked my hand away and took a couple of steps back. I wanted to go into the bathroom and collect myself, but I couldn't trust that my words had gotten through to her. And so, I breathed deeply and waited for her to come back to me, also waiting on my own self to return.

Gwyn burst into tears, and I didn't so much as flinch. The scene rang too many cracked bells to tug at my heartstrings. Still, a moth struck a strand as fine as quicksilver, as light as the contour feathers of a finch, and I lowered to rest on a knee.

"Hey."

This time, my call held no beckon. If anything, it was a plea.

"Stay." I said, keeping my arms at my sides, "Rest. Please."

In response, Gwyn tilted her head and cocked an eyebrow, clearly intent on rejecting my condescending tone. I braced myself for her scathing words, but none came. She opened her mouth as if to speak but closed it abruptly before glancing away and then turning to face me directly. The scene played out in an instant, but not a moment was lost on me.

“Fine.” Gwyn said and then took a deep breath in through her nose and breathed out through her mouth. “Okay… Thank you.”

I hesitated only briefly before grinning at her. She smiled back at me, though, she tucked her chin in an attempt to hide it. I didn’t waste time searching for more words. Instead, I stood and made my way to the kitchen.

“You hungry?” I asked.

“I don’t think I could eat right now.” Came the reply.

“What about a salad or some ramen?” I pressed.

There was a pause and then she said, “It’s Ramen.”

She pronounced it “ray-men” and I cringed. I was pretty sure the correct pronunciation was “raw-men”. Hoping to keep her from speaking that grating word again, I moved on.

Unfortunately, the most substantial thing in my fridge was a hand grenade. Next was some spoiled milk and a few vegetables. I let the door swing shut and sighed, knowing that my cabinets were equally vacant. Despite my offer to Gwyn, I didn't want Ramen either. Just to put something in my stomach, I grabbed a bag of potato chips and returned to the living room.

"I'm not really that hungry either." I sat the bag of chips on the floor between us. "But we should probably eat at least a little."

She slid out of the recliner and joined me on the floor. As we munched on chips, it occurred to me that she never told me why she was in the cop car. I glanced at her, wondering what sort of trouble she had been in.

"So," I said, brushing the salt from my fingers and trying to sound nonchalant, "What were you doing in the back of that car?"

She froze with a chip inches from her lips. I thought she might shoot me a glare and tell me it was none of my business. But she just lowered her hand and hung her head, as if in shame. I sensed that whatever she had done, she was not proud of it, and I quickly spoke up, still trying to sound casual.

"You don't have to tell me. I was just curious."

She didn't meet my eyes, but she did tell me. I won't put her words here. They were private and they will remain that way. Suffice it to say that people go through hard times, and they make bad decisions.

By the time she finished her telling, tears streaked her face faster than she could wipe them away. She wrapped her arms around her knees and kept her head down as she sobbed. Unlike before, the sight broke my heart. I felt tears running down my own face and had to swallow hard before I could speak. Even still, all I got out was a choked "Gwyn" before I realized that there was nothing to be said. So, I moved closer, put my arms around her, and held her against my chest as she cried herself to sleep.

I sat there for a while after she drifted off, trying to sort through everything I was feeling. The night had been an emotional roller coaster for the record books. I had seen people killed, killed others, saved an ex-girlfriend, been saved by an ex-girlfriend, shit my pants twice (another record?) and, of course, zombies were the cause of it all. I shook my head at the turn of events and thought "Eh. What can ya do?"

I chuckled at the voice of an old rabbi in my head and made to pick Gwyn up. Her eyes shot open as soon as I shifted, and she sat up rubbing at her face. I watched her confusion drain away as she focused on me.

"Sorry." She said, still trying to rub dried tears from her face.

I reached out and took her hands in my own. I leaned forward to place a kiss on her forehead and smiled at her as I stood.

I said, "I think it's bed time."

She nodded tiredly in response and let me pull her to her feet. I offered my bed and she readily accepted, though, she insisted I sleep next to her. I tried to be a gentleman but my desire to lie next to a beautiful woman won over. There was no intimacy beyond the way she held my hand and cuddled up to me. In spite of everything that had happened, I slept better than I had in a long time.

Chapter 5

When I woke, sunlight was shining in through the slightly sheer curtains and Gwyn was gone. I sat up abruptly and looked around the room. She was gone. My heart started racing and I dragged the blankets off of the bed in my haste to stand. Then, over my panicked grunts, I heard the toiled flush.

A relieved sigh left me in a rush, and I lay back down, fixing the mess I'd made. Gwyn strode silently into the room a minute later and rejoined me under the blankets. She looked tired and reinforced that image by putting her back to me and pulling my arm around her, apparently intent on going back to sleep.

"I thought you left." I said.

She half turned over and glanced at me sideways, “Why would I leave?”

I shrugged. “You’ve just always done your own thing.”

She chewed her lip a moment before matching my shrug and resting her head on the pillow again, “I don’t really know what to do. I don’t even know where I am.”

I frowned. “What? Don’t you live around here?”

A pause. I started to wonder if she’d fallen asleep when she shook her head slightly and said, “No.”

My frown deepened into puzzlement. “You still live in Bliss then?”

Instead of answering, she sat up and tossed the blankets aside.

“I’m hungry”, was all she said before standing and making her way to the kitchen.

I watched her go and sighed; sure I’d said something to upset her. I had no idea what it might have been, but I mentally added another tally to my list of failed social interactions before rolling out of bed and making my way to the kitchen.

I didn't have much aside from some lettuce, tomatoes, and cucumbers but the shredded cheese and vinaigrette shaped it into a semblance of a meal. We washed it down, water for me, milk for her, and settled down in front of the TV with a fresh bowl of weed.

"But the cause is still unknown," The news anchor was saying. "Rhonda Bloom, director of the Centers for Disease Control and Prevention, had this to say."

The image changed to a view of a harried looking woman in her mid forties. She wore a green pantsuit with a dingy blouse beneath her wrinkled jacket. A single microphone rose from the podium in front of her and two large, black suited bodyguards stood behind, looking nearly as disheveled as their charge. The audio faded in.

"Our main focus at this time is containing the disease. As of yet, there is no clear indication as to the cause of the outbreak. We…" The director's jaw clenched, and she swallowed hard before continuing, "Every available member of our team is working on a way to treat the infected. Until further notice, avoid quarantined areas, stay inside your homes at all costs, and do not attempt to reach loved ones…"

She trailed off, her eyes drifting down from the cameras. Several seconds passed before they snapped back into focus. Wordlessly, she turned from the podium and hurried off-screen, a guard in front and a guard behind. A shot of the empty stage lingered for a few moments before the image shifted back to the local anchor.

"Director Bloom has not been heard from since that briefing which took place at six a.m. eastern time." Swiveling to look into a different camera, she continued, "Numerous terrorist groups have taken credit for the outbreak of what is now being called the Pelios virus."

A graphic appeared over the anchor's shoulder; a map of the United States covered in red to show the "hot zones". The screen went black, and I flinched as if I'd been slapped. Whipping my head around, I turned to face Gwyn. She held the TV remote limply in one hand and stared blankly at the blank screen, as if she could see past it and through the wall behind.

"We're going to die."

Her monotone near-whisper seemed to pass her lips unbeknownst to her. I sat next to her in silence for a while before saying anything.

"Yeah," I said, nodding easily, "We are."

She turned and met my eyes, a look of fearful sadness creeping onto her face. I shrugged it away.

"We will die. Everybody dies, Gwyn." I paused before leaning over and resting my hand on her arm, "But we're not dead yet."

Instead of inspiring, my morbid optimism seemed to upset her even more. I pulled my hand back as she dropped the remote and brought both hands to her face, failing in her attempt to suppress her tears. I chewed my lip, wishing I could make everything better for her, even just a little.

"Hey," I said after a while, trying to sound conversational, "How do you think Tyler would handle all of this?"

I thought I sensed a slight hesitation in her posture before she suddenly chuckled into her hands, "He wouldn't be crying like a little bitch."

I raised an eyebrow, easily imagining our old friend curled up into a ball and weeping quietly in a closet. He wasn't weak but he was emotional. I didn't argue the point.

I smiled and said, "I can almost see it. He'd have already stolen a military helicopter and a truckload of guns. He'd be halfway to Florida, intent on claiming Universal Studios. The CDC would have to contain him before they could worry about the virus."

She actually laughed.

* * *

Everything from the cop cars, blankets and pillows, clothes, toiletries, trash bags, plus some random odds and ends, all made the list.

I replaced Gary's collar with a harness and watched amusedly as he did his dance. He was actually excited to go outside. I couldn't tell if he didn't remember what had happened or if he just didn't give a shit. Absently, I thought of how everyone seemed to think I would take care of things. I sighed, brandished the shotgun, and pushed the couch out of the way.

Leaning against the door with my fingers splayed like a spider's legs, I peered out once more through the peephole. A zombie stood inches from the door, so close that I could see its irises. They stood stark against its blood-smeared face. Not white, I noticed. Its eyes were powder blue and would have been beautiful on anyone else.

My breath left me in one hard exhale and the zombie cocked its head to the side as if listening. I froze. I stopped breathing, stopped blinking. I tried to stop my heart from beating. Then, moving slower than cheese though my intestines, I stepped away from the door and leveled the shotgun.

When nothing happened, I bent to pick up Gary and gestured toward the bedroom. I followed her in and closed the door behind us. The sight of the zombie cocking its head played over and over in my head. Finally, Gwyn spoke softly.

"What is it?"

I shook my head and whispered. "It's one…" I worked some moisture into my mouth and tried again. "There's one out there."

She asked evenly, "What are we gonna do?"

I thought for a moment. She waited for me to respond but I was lost in thought. A few minutes later, I was standing on my balcony with a gun in my hand. Not the shotgun. I didn't want to fall over the rail while trying to shoot at an awkward angle. With Gwyn prepared to push the couch back in front of the door, I set the plan, such as it was, into motion.

Speaking just loudly enough for the shithead around the corner to hear me, I said, "Heeeeeere pigpigpigpig. Heeeeeere pig…"

I was cut off by a choking snarl. I cocked my gun and waited for it to come hauling ass around the corner or, better yet, fall head first down the stairs. Neither of those things happen. Nothing happened. The snarling continued but no monsters came running out. I leaned out over the rail but couldn't see more than a few steps up.

I said, "Hey." Then louder, "Hey! Bear fucker!"

A cry rose from the breezeway. It wasn't quite the same as the battle cries I had heard the night before. But it wasn't exactly a sad cry and it sure as shit wasn't a happy one either. For a minute, I considered the possibility that it knew about the trap. Then I remembered how fences, doors, and stairs had stumped the other ones and tossed that idea away. Except…

I leaned in through the doorway and waved Gwyn over. With reluctance, she got up from the couch, I'd told her to sit on it once she got it back in place and joined me on the balcony.

I whispered, "Start talking like you're confused and lost."

Her face scrunched in bemusement. "Why?"

I drew my lips into a line. I didn't want to discuss it. I just wanted to kill the fucking zombie that thought it could trap me. The zombie that was waiting for my door to open so it could murder me.

"Just trust me."

With a skeptical glare, she began, "Hello? Is someone there?"

I nodded and whispered, "Lean out and face the parking lot."

She did as much, saying, "Please. I heard someone. What's happening? Where is everyone?"

Soon there was a roar followed by the sound of a zombie falling down some stairs. I smiled and prepared to let loose on the bastard. In the second that it took for it to come into view, my smile faltered at the realization that this zombie was smart enough to resist my outright taunting. Then something else happened.

Gwyn threw her arms over her ears as the zombie fell into the sunlight and began to howl. It's shrieking wails were like nails on a chalkboard amplified a thousand times, distilled, and jammed into your ears with a syringe. I struggled to pull the trigger through the pain and managed a wild spasm of a shot. It took the fucker in the chest and, though it didn't stop flailing, it's screams devolved into gurgling coughs.

I stared in wonder as its flesh became flaky and ashen. It wasn't burning so much as peeling. It was as if it had been covered in clear wax that had dried to be brittle. Beneath the flakes, almost scales, was the pink flesh of a newborn baby.

"What the fuck?"

It was Gwyn who had spoken. For some reason, whenever she uttered that short rhetorical question, something occurred to me that probably already should have. I half turned to go back inside before leaning back out over the rail and putting another round in the zombie. I didn't know if whatever was happening would kill it, but I didn't want to risk it crawling to safety.

I hurried back inside and turned the TV to the local news. Immediately, a voice came through and Gwyn and I exchanged uneasy glances at what was being said by the woman wearing too much makeup.

"… advised to stay indoors at all costs. The attackers are fast and strong and have very good hearing. Any attempts to contact the attackers is strictly prohibited, as there seems to be an infectious element at play. Again, all in the area are advised to stay indoors at all costs…"

"Holy shit." I sighed. "God damn it." Then, to Gwyn's surprise as well as my own, I began to laugh. As usual, it started small and then quickly grew into great bellows of laughter before graduating to silent wheezes of near hysteria. At Gwyn's confused and slightly unsettled expression, I explained.

"I've always wanted something like this to happen." I said, still reeling from my jollity, "You'd think I'd regret it now that everything's all fucked. But I don't. I think it's fucking hilarious."

Ignoring thoughts of the dead, I threw my head back in laughter once again and, for a time, forgot about the knot that had been forming in my stomach. Gwyn stared at me for a few more seconds before a smile cracked her mask of concern and she began to laugh with me. We cackled madly together for a good while before getting back down to business.

She wiped her eyes and asked, "Did it know you were trying to draw it out?"

I shook my head but not to answer in the negative. "I think it did on a certain level. I think it was trying to stay out of the sun. When I started quoting movies at it from around the corner, the fear of going out into the sun was enough to keep it from diving down the stairs in pursuit. But it wasn't enough once it heard a scared woman, apparently too stupid to run away, basically delivering herself to it."

I noticed her expression and realized I had stated my theory as if I were Madame Curie discovering radium. I felt my face redden and I suddenly felt like I'd dumped my porn collection at her feet. I wasn't aroused by my musings to any degree. I did, however, find the idea of a potential caste system amongst zombies to be fascinating. It suggested something about our future that I didn't particularly care to think on.

"So…" Gwyn said tentatively, "What does that mean? Can we go out now?"

I studied her face and remembered our goal. I couldn't just stay there and ponder the inner workings of my enemy. We had to get moving if we wanted to survive. The good news was that the zombies appeared to be vampiric in the sense that they didn't fare well in direct sunlight.

"I think we can go out. As long as we stay out of the shadows, we'll probably be safe."

Gwyn watched me for a moment and said, "You're almost autistic sometimes."

I felt the beginnings of a bristling at her comment but shrugged it off.

"I'll take that as a compliment, meh lady." I bowed with a flourish as I imagined so many lords once did for their lieges.

She let loose a tinkling giggle and I found myself easily forgetting the offense I had almost taken. With a grin, I met her eyes and asked, “Are you ready?”

She answered by stroking her pistol and winking at me. I shook my head with an easy grin on my face and moved once more to peer through the peephole. Gary sat patiently in the corner, waiting for providence to take hold.

By the grace of God, there weren’t any fucking zombies standing century outside. I unlocked the door and stepped confidently through. That confidence was quickly demolished by the zombie that leapt down the half-flight of stairs to my right and was recovering with the clear intent to close the distance. All it had to do was shift its hips and lunge and I would have been grappling with it on the wooden planks.

Before I could so much as flinch, a gunshot popped in my ear and the zombie went stumbling over the rail. It clipped the railing below on its way down and landed awkwardly. Its shoulder was dislocated to the point of wanting to rip free and blood flowed liberally from a gash across the forehead. Additionally, it landed in sunlight from the waist up.

The shrieking howls began again, and I stumbled back inside with my hands over my ears, kicking the door shut behind me. I snatched a cushion from the couch and shoved Gwyn into the bathroom, kicking that door shut as well. We huddled in the bathtub until the howls degraded into barely audible whimpering.

With a start, I searched the small bathroom. I didn't see Gary. Almost tossing Gwyn aside, I bounded from the tub and flung the door open. Gary lay knotted in a terrified ball just outside.

I felt like a shithead. I almost turned and asked Gwyn to shoot me in the foot, right then. The thought truly crossed my mind. My guy was alone through that mess. I had closed the door on him and hadn't even noticed in the rush to save myself and Gwyn. I felt an irrational resentment rise up within me and I sent a barely veiled glare over my shoulder as I knelt to pick him up.

"Hey, buddy." I said soothingly, "It's alright, little guy. You're a good boy, buddy. Yeah, it's okay."

"I'm fine." Gwyn said scathingly, "Thanks for slamming my head into the wall."

"I'm sorry." I didn't sound sorry. "Gary's my guy and I…"

I trailed off and shot her another glare. "You have to help me watch him. He needs us more than we need each other."

She just stared at me with a bemused look on her face as I rocked Gary back and forth like a baby. He was shaking and I was sure he was doing it just to make me feel worse than I already did. I sat down in the doorway and let him go so he wouldn't feel trapped. He walked in a quick circle then nestled into my side and kept his head buried in my lap, still trembling.

Gwyn said, "You'd be a good father."

The words struck a plethora of fractured strands within my nerves. I stiffened at once. My relationship with Gary, my relationship with the plants growing in pots on my balcony and the road kill that cropped up with regularity on my way to work; these were all things for which I cared greatly. But I was no father. I'd sooner become a scarecrow, especially considering the sudden end of so-called "civilized society". The world was no place for a person.

Forcing a shrug I said, "I'm just that kind of awesome."

She rolled her eyes and then seemed to consider throwing the little green bar of soap at me. I half flinched before she relaxed her arm and made to stand from the tub. I stood as well, and we made our way back into the living room.

I knelt to pick Gary up and realized how ridiculous that was. I was going to, what, face the zombies with my dog in one arm and a shotgun in the other? I'm not from that far south, alright? I'm my own man. That's why I ended up walking down the middle of the street with Gwyn on my six and Gary strapped to my back. To my delight, he seemed to like his position and held still, perched as he was, panting easily.

There were bodies everywhere. I would tell it differently but there is no substitute for the simple truth. A full half of the residents within a square mile must have been clustered around my apartment complex. There were no piles beyond the tangles of three or four at the base of each set of stairs we passed, but hundreds lay dead across the manicured lawns and untended ditches.

"Why are they staring at us?"

I turned and said, "Who?"

She gestured toward the nearest apartments, and I followed the motion. What I saw made me wonder why Gwyn hadn't started shouting yet.

“Holy shit.” I hissed.

“What?” Gwyn replied, trying to look in every direction at once.

I recovered quickly and turned to face her. Either she had balls of steel, or she couldn’t see what I could. After seeing the way, she squinted at her surroundings, I removed my glasses and offered them to her.

“Isn’t this bad for my eyes?” She asked as she dawned the narrow spectacles.

“Yeah.” I said simply, “It is. Just look at the buildings and then take them off.”

Settling the lenses in front of her eyes, she turned and took in the scenery. With a choking gasp, she flung my glasses back at me and grabbed my arm. In spite of my discomfort at being leered at by the undead, a smile crept onto my face as I snatched my glasses out of the air.

“Holy shit!” Gwyn shouted, “What the fuck, Van? What the fuck?”

“Careful.” I admonished, “If these break then we’re both blind.”

I held up my glasses then huffed on them and set to cleaning them on my shirt. Of course, my shirt was already sweaty and only served to further smear my lenses. Sighing at the headache that would surely come on from straining to see through the smudges, I slid them back onto my face and continued down the street.

"I think we should take the ambulance." Gwyn said, looking increasingly anxious about being out in the open.

"We're going to." I continued to scan the streets and buildings. "I just wanted to see."

She tugged on my arm, and I let her lead me back to the parking lot. The people in the windows and doorways were all zombies, of course. Most of them were injured to different degrees. Some of them pressed their bloody half-naked bodies against glass like undead hookers in a Rob Zombie production of a red-light district. Others simply stood or crouched. But each and every one of them stared at us with psychotic hunger in their eyes.

The sight would haunt my dreams for several nights.

"Come on." Gwyn urged me, "I don't want to be here anymore."

I nodded and jogged with her to the ambulance. Before going, we checked the cop cars again. There were a few more flares in Sean's trunk as well as another shotgun and a box of shells. I considered checking the officers for supplies as well, but I didn't want to see their bodies, let alone lute them.

After checking the cab for zombies and finding none, we loaded up and took off. I weaved between bodies as my home disappeared behind me. After the night I'd just had there, I was relieved when we hit the highway and headed north, away from home and toward the only other place I could think to go, The pizza parlor.

Chapter 6

Corpses and abandoned vehicles littered the streets. Clusters of men, women, and children lay everywhere. Inside many of the vehicles, the occupants slumped over their steering wheels or halfway out of their open doors. A large portion of the vehicles were well into the surrounding fields as if they'd all veered off of the road at full speed without ever braking, only stopping when they crashed.

The two-mile drive took fifteen minutes at our careful pace. Many more abandoned cars lined up at the intersection next to the shop. Bodies hunched over steering wheels inside almost all of them. I had to drive over the curb to get into the parking lot, but we were soon parked next to the front entrance.

"Are we going in?" Gwyn asked, trying to see past the reflective surface of the storefront.

"I'd like to." I said, "There's lots of food and drink in there."

I also wanted to see if any of my coworkers were inside, but I didn't think that necessary to bring up. The supplies were a good enough reason to go in.

Gwyn nodded and hefted her gun. “I hope there aren’t any…” She trailed off before continuing, “Zombies?”

I shrugged, “That’s what I’ve been calling them.”

She said, “We should try rattling the door or something. Maybe they’ll come out in the open like the other one.”

I nodded my approval, “Sounds good.”

She eyed me for a moment before throwing her door open and stepping out of the truck. I watched her jaunt up to the entrance and knock on the metal frame with her gun. She took a few quick steps back, aiming at the doors.

A zombie came barreling through a second later, shoving a fist through one of the panels of glass in the process. The arm caught on the wicked shards with a sound like a jacket being zipped up. A series of yanks and tugs left the arm in a mess of torn flesh and tendons as the zombie struggled to free itself.

I cursed and made to jump out and help. The edge of the building was keeping the sun from hitting the zombie and it could jump far enough to reach Gwyn if it got free. By the time I reached for the handle, though, the situation had resolved itself. While the zombie mutilated its arm on the door, Gwyn calmly lined up a headshot and blew the fucking thing away. She turned, winked at me, and strolled in through the broken door.

I stared after her, considering how much I wanted her to fuck me on the pizza prep table. Gary whined from his position next to me and I was brought back from my fantasies. I pulled the keys from the ignition and grabbed the shotgun from the floorboard.

Inside the store was total disarray. Bags of chips and candy lay strewn about the tiled floor. Brown, yellow, and blue soda mixed with red blood, forming colorful swirls amid the slain. Two bodies lay face to bloody face, as if they had died kissing or head-butting one another. I didn't recognize them.

"Why is this happening?"

I turned to find Gwyn looking at the bodies as well. She faced them, but her eyes seemed to stare beyond the scene of violent death. I didn't answer, not knowing what to say.

"I could almost believe this is all a bad trip." She went on, "This just seems so…"

I waited.

"It's like someone just flipped a switch and suddenly everything was fucked up." She said, "I keep expecting to wake up."

I raised an eyebrow. "That's a good way to put it. I'm pretty sure we aren't sleeping or tripping, though."

Gwyn opened her mouth to say something but cut off as a sound came from the back of the store. We spun around but didn't see anything. Gwyn headed toward the sound. I stopped her with a hand on her shoulder. She glanced at me questioningly and I held up a finger.

"Hello?" I hollered, "Leslie? Abby? It's me, Van."

We waited for a response, but none came. Quickly scanning the darkened store, we made our way into the kitchen. The entire back floor looked like a giant pizza. It was covered in both blood and marinara sauce as well as all of the accoutrements; pepperoni and green peppers, mushrooms, olives, chives.

Gwyn stared at the floor and then said, "What a splendid pie."

I grinned, “I was just thinking that.”

We spun on our heels as a muted thud came from the walk-in freezer. I eased up to the thick door and rested my ear against it. Faint rustling sounded inside, so quiet I almost missed it. Motioning for Gwyn to stand behind me, I reached out a fist and knocked ‘shave and a haircut, two bits’.

Not getting a response, I nodded at Gwyn and then at the door. She gave me a doubtful look. I held my gun in one hand and used the other to pantomime her opening the door and me shooting whatever came out. Reluctantly, she moved to the door and rested her hand on the lever. The heavy door put up a fight, but the petite woman managed to wrangle it open.

Boxes of cheese, lunch meat and produce were stacked just inside, as if placed there intentionally. Frowning, I peered over the top, noticing that the A/C wasn’t blowing any cold air even though it was warmer than usual in there. I also noticed a stack of boxes to the right and a person wedged in between two shelves behind them. I cocked my head. I couldn’t see their face, but I could see part of their chest. It was heaving with the motions of gasping breaths.

“Hey.” I said, trying to sound disarming, “Are you okay?”

For a moment, the heaving chest fell still.

“We’re not going to hurt you.” I went on, “It’s okay to come out.”

“Van?”

I sighed in relief. The voice belonged to one of my coworkers. I could hear the trembling in her voice as she spoke my name.

“Hey, Eliza. Yeah, it’s me. I’ve got a friend with me too. It’s alright to come out.”

She craned her neck so I could see her face. She closed her eyes and shook her head, making no motions to leave her small fort. I chewed my lip and glanced at Gwyn. She was watching Eliza with a mixture of concern and disapproval. Mostly disapproval. I frowned at her and nudged her with my elbow. She just rolled her eyes and started back toward the front of the store.

“You know,” I said, turning back toward Eliza, “Those zombie things sort of burn in the sunlight. You’re probably safer outside than inside right now. Plus, we have a few guns. We could give you one. Those things are fast and strong, but they aren't bullet proof."

I smiled, hoping to seem optimistic but probably just looking like a bloodthirsty psychopath. Fortunately, Eliza and I had worked together for over two years. She was used to my failed attempts at socializing.

She didn't return my smile, but she did crawl out of the freezer. I helped her to her feet and reached into the small of my back to retrieve my sidearm. I held it out and then hesitated.

"You know how to use this right? I mean, you aren't going to accidentally shoot one of us or yourself if you get scared are you?"

She gave me a flat look. "Van, I hunt every year. We've talked about it several times. You've seen my dad's gun collection."

I held up my hands in surrender. "Alright, alright."

She sighed, "I'm sorry. I've been in that freezer all night. Someone banged on the door the whole time and I thought I was going to die. I had to break the fan to keep from freezing."

She stared at the ground for a minute, seeming to see more than the tiles. Abruptly, she straightened her back, squared her shoulders, and extended a hand. I placed the gun in it and watched as she examined the small weapon with a smooth efficiency. I had never been attracted to Eliza before, not really, but seeing her pull herself together and then handle that gun the way she did gave me a few new ideas.

"Do you have your car?" She asked.

"We have an ambulance." I said proudly.

She cocked an eyebrow. "How did you get an ambulance?"

"We had a bad night, too." I said and then hesitated, "I don't really want to talk about it."

"Fair enough," She said, "Two more questions: Where are you going, and can I come with you?"

I chuckled. "You can come with us, but I have no idea where we're going."

She looked a little unsettled at our lack of a plan, but only for a moment. "We can go out to my house. It's outside of town so there probably won't be any…"

“Just say it.” I said, shrugging, “Unless you have a better word.”

“…Zombies.” She finished. “There probably won’t be any zombies out there.” She let out a humorless chuckle. “My parents are probably worried about me too. I hope Colby got home okay.”

The last seemed to be said to herself. Colby was her fiancé. I had only seen him a handful of times. Each time, he seemed like a nice enough guy. However, I got the feeling that he was into some of the harder stuff. Namely meth. He always struck me as one of those tweakers who thinks that shooting up is okay just so long as they wait until the weekend to do it. Still, he seemed nice.

“I’m sure they’re all fine.” I said, “Like you said, they’re way outside of town so they probably didn’t have to deal with all of this.”

I made a gesture that took in the mess around us. She nodded in agreement, but her expression was still guarded. I waved at her to follow and led the way back up front. Gwyn had already found a hand truck and was loading up cases of water and soda into the back of the ambulance.

"We should throw some of this stuff out." She called from the box, "We need food and water more than we need this gurney."

Before I could object, she unlocked the wheels and shoved the gurney out of the open doors of the ambulance. It crashed to the ground, tipping over stiffly before coming to a rest on its side. I stared at it and then up at Gwyn. She wasn't even paying attention to me.

"Hey." I said, "Can we talk about this sort of thing first?"

She fixed me with flat look. I threw my arms out and returned the look. I didn't really care about the gurney. It might have been useful somehow, but not as useful as food, water, and ammo, and the box was full of small cabinets and drawers that couldn't easily be removed. It was a good idea to remove the gurney. It would've been even better if she would have ran it by me first.

"I don't have to ask for permission."

I screwed my face up. "Who the fuck said that? I just asked you to let me weigh in before you destroy our shit."

“Whoa, dude.” She said, walking past me, “Chill. It’s just a gurney.”

The look on her face said that I was flying off the handle for no reason. I gritted my teeth and resolved to either kill her right then or keep my mouth shut. I remained silent. Eliza stood to the side through the power struggle, looking like she might just go back into the freezer for a while.

After a few deep breaths and some internal “woosahs”, I gave Eliza a resigned look and went to help Gwyn gather supplies. She hesitated, probably deciding whether or not to let herself get mixed up in our mess within a disaster. In the end, I figured it was the fear of being alone that made her come back in to help. Either way, I had gained another companion, a survivor, and I was feeling good about it.

Chapter 7

Once we had gathered every bit that seemed prudent, we set out. Cans of mushrooms and olives along with boxes of chips and bottles of soda and water settled on the axel and we headed toward the sticks.

Eliza's family did indeed live out of town. After a half hour drive through forest and farmland, we came to a private road of dirt and gravel. Half way up the winding goat-path of a road, I came to a stop and suggested we walk the rest of the way in order to save the tires. Gwyn had some objections but ultimately, grudgingly, she agreed.

The walk was easy enough, if uphill. Tall grasses lined either side of the narrow drive. The golden fields reminded me of pleasant mornings in my home town. Those early days that started with bare feet in damp grass and ended with a filthy, smiling boy being herded into the shower. The thought almost made me smile, but it only took a few minutes to reach the house and, as it came into view, Eliza spoke up.

"They're all home." Her face flashed with relief, "I'm surprised they didn't come looking for me, though."

I shared a quick look with Gwyn. "They probably knew you'd be alright." I said, adding, "And that it'd be fucking stupid to leave this place."

Eliza nodded faintly, but her relief had been replaced by worry. After all, her family hadn't come looking for her. In her mind, they were either dead or they didn't care enough to risk saving her. I took a few more steps before turning to face her.

"El? You alright?"

She met my eyes but didn't respond. Her gaze flicked to Gwyn, then at her house, then back at me. I kept my face impassive. Without looking away, I tilted my head toward the large, Victorian-style house.

"You ready?"

Sadness teased at her face for a few broken seconds before she recovered. Eliza was smart. She was smart enough to know what I was thinking, at least. She knew the odds too. More than anything, she knew she couldn't turn away from this. She held my gaze and nodded.

I had the sudden fear that we would find her whole family as zombies. I was sure we could handle them, though, I hesitated at the thought of Eliza plugging me execution-style for shooting her undead loved ones.

I glanced at Gwyn, trying to figure out how to communicate my concerns with just my eyebrows. Thankfully, she had already drawn the same conclusions. She gave a firm nod that said she would have my back. Slightly relieved, I moved forward with my shotgun trained on the door.

"Be careful." Eliza said, reaching out and holding my arm.

I glanced at her hand. "I'll be careful." I promised, knowing that she was worried about me shooting her fiancé. I was worried about not shooting a big enough hole in him when he tried to eat my face. It was awkward, lying to her in that way. I felt unclean.

She released my arm, and I tried to give her a reassuring look. Without further ado, I twisted the brass knob and pushed the antique door open. The hinges groaned as I stepped inside.

"Colby." Eliza called out, "Mom, dad?"

We paused briefly and listened for a response, but none came. We shared glances, all on guard for our own reasons, and moved in. Just inside and to the left was the kitchen. I was surprised by how messy it was. Then I realized that all of the food sitting out was in preparation for a large meal that was never finished. Cans of dehydrated milk lay next to a can opener and a carton of eggs. A bag of flour had fallen from the counter and shot its load across the floor.

I turned to face Eliza, hoping she was looking anywhere but the kitchen. She was looking at me, actually. Well, she was looking over my shoulder and with wide, horrified eyes. I heard a low, breathy moan and felt a rumbling in my gut. Before I could shit my pants again, I spun on my heel, prepared to shoot.

"No!" Eliza yelled.

I felt her hand tug at my arm. There was a grunt and the hand fell away. I could faintly hear Gwyn muttering behind me, but my attention was locked on the figure coming down the hall. I'd seen some crazy shit by this point, but I still wasn't prepared for what I saw entering the room now.

It was definitely a zombie. No doubt about that. Unless, of course, it was a demon. He was completely naked and had a massive, bloody erection. Instead of running me down like all of the others had tried, he hunched over while somehow leaning back and walked with his legs out in front of him, his arms hanging at his sides. He sauntered, and he smiled easily.

If it wasn't enough having Shaggy from Scooby-Doo point at me with his lacerated dick, in his right hand he held by a fistful of dark hair what I assumed to be both his fuck-toy and the severed head of Eliza's father. The mutilated dome piece dripped brains and bloody cum as it swung through the air.

I stood, frozen in shock. This said things about whatever was changing people that made me want to turn my gun on myself. For a moment, I considered the possibility that he wasn't a zombie. If I tried, I could almost believe that he'd acquired some bad meth and just snapped. Almost.

Fighting the rising urge to vomit, I took a step forward, raised the shotgun, and put a hole in his chest. The shot flung him backward and into a wall. The severed head flew from his grasp, soaring past me to land with a wet smack on the tiled floor amid the spilled flour.

The boom of the shotgun set my ears ringing but I recovered quickly. The large house diffused the sound of the explosion well. I turned and saw Gwyn on the ground with Eliza. Eliza was unconscious and Gwyn was tending to her.

"What happened?" I asked, kneeling next to them.

"Exactly what we thought would happen." She spoke softly and stroked Eliza's hair with a gentle touch.

I looked at her, confused by both her words and her tenderness toward this woman who was a stranger to her. The image of that next-level rapist was still fresh in my mind, too, and it was difficult to think of anything else, but I'd never seen Gwyn be gentle like that before.

“Is she okay?” I asked.

Gwyn nodded and said, “She’ll have a headache. Hopefully a little bit of memory loss but probably not. I didn’t hit her that hard.”

“You hit her? Why?”

Gwyn’s mouth formed into a line as she glared up at me. “I thought that was why you wanted me in the back. She was going to try to stop you and save her zombie family. So, yeah, I hit her. She’ll wake up in a minute or two. Fucking chill, dude.”

I screwed my face up. “Damn, man. You fucking chill.”

Belatedly, I added, “Thank you.”

She let out a huff of a sigh and turned her attention back to Eliza. I stood and began searching the house. Eliza’s mom could be anywhere and in any state of need, from bandages to bullets. After the condition we found her fiancé in, I wasn’t psyched about the idea of seeking her out. I could just imagine walking in on an old zombie woman stuffing her cunt with a severed fist—

This time, I didn't fight it. I leaned over and vomited in one of the large potted plants in the living room. Gwyn gave me a pitying look. I spit in the pot and then scooted it to the far end of the living room, feeling much better.

I replaced the expended shell in my gun and edged down the hallway, checking each room in turn. It took nearly half an hour to search all of them. Eventually, unfortunately, I found Mrs. Sulle in the last place I thought to look.

She lay in the sunroom, shriveled like a dried worm. All around her body lay scale-like flakes of the dried goop. I stood, staring at the corpse for a long while. A hand on my arm brought me out of my trance.

Startled, I turned and found Eliza, not Gwyn, standing next to me. I moved as if to shield her from seeing but she just grabbed my arm and led me away from the small sunlit patio.

"I'm sorry, El." I felt defeated, like I'd failed her. I thought to say more but could form no words.

She looked at me, the unshed tears in her eyes eager to follow the streams running down her sun-weathered face. For a moment, I thought she would fall to the floor and just give up, ask me to end it for her. It's what I would have done. Instead, her expression of loss gradually faded into a look of resolve. She took a deep breath and guided me back through the house.

Her eyes drifted down and fixed onto her slain fiancé as we passed him in the hallway. With a quavering voice, she said, "I won't just lay down and die when I know they would have wanted me to keep going."

I was taken aback by her fervor, by her fire. A part of me was certain that she was repressing an unhealthy amount of emotion. But another part of me said that there was nothing to do but bury the dead and continue living, apocalypse or no. Above it all, she inspired me, and I told her as much.

Her tightlipped smile, just the hint of a grin, was one of the most amazing things I'd ever seen. It frightened me and filled me with uncertainty about my own potential. It was humbling to witness. I stared at her with my mouth hanging open until Gwyn appeared at my side.

"So, what do we now? With them." Gwyn stared at the floor, avoiding meeting Eliza's eyes.

I glanced at her, both disturbed and relieved that someone else had asked the question. I offered to take the bodies outside and bury them in the yard. I had already seen the entire horror show and none of them were my family. I insisted. Gwyn was more than pleased to leave me to it and go pack up supplies instead. Eliza, however, insisted right back at me.

I'd say, "They're your family, El. You shouldn't have to see them like that."

And she would say, "Exactly, they're my family. I'm doing this."

I put up only a weak fight. I wasn't about to deny her will. It was her family, her home. She didn't stop me from helping though.

We took our time removing the bodies. Not only was our duty solemn, but we didn't know how infectious the sickness was. I had seen Officer Dan change after only being tackled. So, we wrapped them in sheets without touching them.

I suggested that Eliza decide where to bury them and asked where I could find a shovel. I half turned and took a step away, expecting her to point me toward the shed. When she only continued to stare at her linen wrapped loved ones, I leaned against the wall and waited.

After a while, she said, “They loved this house.”

“It’s a beautiful house.” I said.

She smiled a tight smile and nodded. Her smile firmed into a grin, but the light of memory still shone in her eyes.

“I grew up here just like my parents. I have memories in this house that I sometimes think might actually just be things I’ve seen in movies.” An easier smile briefly flashed across her face before fading. “My family was beautiful, and we lived a good life together. But it’s all over now.”

I looked at her sharply, “It’s not over, El.”

“I don’t mean it like that.” She said, shaking her head. “They’re gone and our life together is over. My home is just as dead. I’d like to bury it with them.”

I looked at her, unable to keep a few tears from escaping my eyes. I opened my mouth to ask what she meant but it clicked before I could.

The house was beautiful, but it was not my home. And, in spite of the utility of the old Victorian-style structure, I knew that Eliza needed closure. I sounded more opposed to the idea than I actually felt whenever I spoke.

“You want to burn your house down?”

She didn’t seem to notice my recrimination. Her eyes never left the forms at her feet. When she finally spoke, she didn’t mince words.

“Yes, I do.”

Chapter 8

I couldn't think of any good reasons not to burn Eliza's house down. I did, however, suggest that she take some things with her. Not just mementos, but whatever she thought might come in handy. I knew she had a great bong collection, for one thing. Also, she had a cat. I'd seen a feline nose peering out from under a bed during my search. We couldn't just light a match and be done with it.

I found Gwyn sitting on the front porch, eating a can of sliced pears. Her expression was distant as I strode over to join her. The spoon she had gotten from the kitchen was resting in her mouth, the handle held loosely in her hand. She flinched slightly and her eyes came into focus as I began to speak.

"Eliza wants to put all of this behind her. After this mess, there's no way we could stay here anyway. So, we're going to burn the house down."

I delivered the words as if they were a eulogy. I had resigned myself to not knowing how she would respond. Part of me thought she would scorn the waste. But I couldn't be sure with her. I prepared myself for a struggle. And so it was that Gwyn's response came as yet another surprise. Looking back, it probably should not have been so shocking.

She slapped her can of pears down on the rail and stood, saying, "Oh my god, yes! Let's do it. I'm ready."

I held up my hands to forestall her. "We're going to get some more stuff and make sure there aren't any animals in the house first." I paused, noticing her eager eyes, "Also, I think Eliza should be the one to start the fire…"

She gave me an impatient look and brushed past me back into the house. As she passed the threshold, I grabbed her forearm and swung her back around to face me. She let out a squawk of surprise and instinctively brought up a hand to hit me. I batted the flailing fist away.

I said, "Come with me."

She let me pull her back outside and lead her down the driveway. The looks she gave, along with the way she switched her hips as she walked, made her assumption of my motives clear. I thought of how she used to like it rough. The open fields made me think of my exhibitionist side. The image of Colby's monster cock, torn and bloody, flashed through my mind and shriveled my mounting arousal like a grape in the sun.

“I didn’t want to walk back down the to the truck alone.” I said, trying to disperse her excitement, “I keep thinking of Colby.”

Her switching stride faltered, and she grimaced.

“That was pretty fucked up.”

I nodded grimly, “I feel bad for Eliza.”

She nodded back and asked. “What happened? Why was he like that?”

I walked silently, replaying Colby’s seductive stride in my head. The look on his face wasn’t rage like I’d seen from the others. The look on his face was pure ecstasy. His eyes had been glazed over, presumably with the prospect of new holes to fuck.

“I don’t know.” I said truthfully, half wondering why she thought I would know but also knowing I wanted to ask the same question of her. “The others were.. angry, I guess. He seemed… excited.”

A hyper Gary, clawing at the windows and shaking with excitement, greeted us at the ambulance. I reached into a pocket for his leash but hesitated. With a quick look around, I opened the door and let him out unfettered. He instantly ran toward Gwyn before banking back in my direction and then finally darting for the fence line.

"Gary!"

The odd tone of my shout confused me for a moment before I realized Gwyn had harmonized with me. For Gary's part, he froze on the spot and crouched low. I let out a sigh of relief and called him back to me. He obeyed, clearly relieved that he wasn't in trouble.

"Stay with me, buddy." I said gently as he approached, "We have to stay together."

He circled me once before resting at my feet like a guard dog. I smiled and bent to scratch his unreasonably large ears. The little guy accepted the praise and didn't move until I started back up the drive.

"What if he runs away?" Gwyn asked. She was watching Gary with a nervous look.

I shook my head, “I’ve had him out without a leash before. He’s only given me trouble once and that was my fault.”

She looked at me questioningly, but I just waved it away. “He’ll be fine. Look how happy he is.”

Gwyn glanced down again and shrugged. “He’s your dog.”

I frowned. Gary was my friend, not my possession. I didn’t own him. I took care of him, and he took care of me. I kept my thoughts silent, not wanting to start an argument over something so small. The silence held until we got back to the house.

Gwyn said, “I should call my parents.”

I stiffened as I remembered my own family a hundred miles to the south. Guilt and anxiety crept over me. The idea should have occurred to me sooner. I wasn’t in the habit of reaching out to my family, but I still cared about them. What if they were hurt, or worse?

I stopped on the front porch, Gwyn behind me and Gary at my side, and tilted my head back, breathing deeply through flared nostrils, trying to slow my thoughts. Honeysuckle vines wove themselves elegantly through the expanse of trellised woodwork overhead. Small white and yellow flowers dotted the lush greenness, looking like clusters of stars in a night sky. Their sweet aroma drifted down through the warm spring air and filled my head with memories.

Pushing the memories away, I lowered my head and turned to face Gwyn. Trying not to smell the flowers, I asked, "Do you think this is happening everywhere?"

She stared intently at the smooth wooden railing as she stroked it with her palm. When she spoke, she sounded bitter.

"Probably."

I clenched my jaw against another wave of emotion and stepped into the house. The heat of the day permeated the old structure and produced waves of the warm, putrid smells of death. The honeysuckle was no match. I pulled the front of my shirt over my nose and then picked Gary up before going upstairs. We found El in her room, coaxing her cat out of the closet.

"Come on, Baba. You can come out. Mamma's here. It's okay, Baba."

Gwyn and I waited at the door, not wanting to further upset Baba. Gwyn arched an eyebrow, and I assumed it was because of the cat's name. I had to agree that it was a silly name. Then again, I guess Gary is sort of an odd name for a dog.

The cat eventually allowed Eliza to scoop her up and we made another trip to the ambulance. Gary was terribly excited to have Baba join our crew. Baba, on the other hand, wasn't quite so eager. With a hiss, the fluff ball leapt from Eliza's arms and took shelter on the high shelves that wrapped around the inside of the truck.

"She'll calm down after a while." Eliza said, rubbing her arm where the frantic cat had scratched her. "I hope."

I sat Gary on the ground and closed the back doors of the ambulance. He stood upright, doing his hominid impersonation as he sniffed in the direction of the cat. I called him away and he went back to doing it doggy style.

We made our way past the fields of shimmering gold and back to the house. Gwyn sat waiting on the porch, smoking a cigarette and swaying slowly in an old rocking chair. Seeing us, she stood, dropping her cigarette and stamping it out on the fine wood.

"Hey." I admonished her, gesturing at the black smear next to her foot. "Don't do that."

"Don't do what?" She shot back, "Don't get ashes on the shit that we're about to set on fire?"

I heard my teeth grinding before I felt it. I said, "It's not shit, Gwyn. And even if it were shit, it wouldn't be your shit. You never fuck…"

"Hey." Eliza cut in, both hands lifted like little walls between us, "It's fine. Let's just do this, okay?"

Still glaring at Gwyn, I said, "You sure you got everything you want to keep?"

Eliza nodded and ran her hand over a fine, silvery necklace that she hadn't been wearing when we arrived. The bands of silver flowed over her collarbones and met at the space between her breasts. In that space, a smooth dark stone wrapped in copper wire rested on her chest just above the spot where her V-shaped collar came to a point.

I opened my mouth but closed it just as quickly. She fingered the stone as she stared distantly, a sad smile on her face. Watching her, I felt as though I knew what she was thinking. She would carry the memory of her family in as well as over her heart and nowhere else. The rest would burn with the dead and remain in the past. Swallowing my suggestion that she save more, I reached into my pocket and proffered my lighter.

Instead of taking it, she seemed to have a thought and abruptly scurried back into the house. I stood, bemused, my arm still extended. Gwyn caught my eye, and I grimaced as I realized how close I'd come to starting a fight with her. I let my arm fall to my side.

"Sorry." I said, "I didn't mean to snap at you. I'm just on edge."

She glanced away and gave a slight shrug but didn't say anything. From her, I expected nothing else. Truces never were her style. I sighed quietly and let it go as I kneeled to scratch behind Gary's ears.

Eliza appeared at the door, and we all turned to look at her. In her hands, she held a small yellow and black container of lighter fluid and a sky-blue Zippo. As she stepped closer, I could see the image of a galloping horse outlined in white across the surface of the lighter.

"That's nice." I offered, "Are you going to keep it?"

She chewed her lip, seeming lost in thought, and answered as if I hadn't spoken.

"My mom made this for my dad when they were teenagers." A smile touched her lips as she continued, "They haven't smoked anything since before I was born, not even weed. But they used to be wild. This lighter has seen some things."

I grinned, having heard some of the stories of David and Lisa Sulle's wild youth. My grin faded as Eliza lifted her head. The unshed tears in her eyes pooled and began to stream down her face. I swallowed against my own tears and moved to see through the door as a flicker of light caught my eye.

Startled, I darted glances at Gwyn and Eliza, "Did you…"

Eliza nodded. Lowering her gaze to her hands again, she turned to face the growing flames inside. We stood silently, none of us sure what to say. I didn't think Eliza wanted to talk very much anyway. Gary gave a soft whine at my feet, and I bent down to pat his head.

A couple of minutes later, Gwyn said, “We should probably go.”

I looked up from Gary and noticed the smoke starting to billow through the top of the open doorway. Eliza took a step closer to her burning home. Taking in some of the thick smoke, she coughed but didn’t step away. I shared a worried glance with Gwyn.

Rising slowly, I said, “El?”

A quick step brought me close to her as she went to her knees. I hesitated as I saw that she was kneeling, not falling. I stepped back to get out of the smoke that was pouring more liberally through the doorway. Stains were beginning to mar the carved wood and flowers alike with violent streaks of black.

Gwyn, looking wary of the growing heat, began retreating down the path. I stayed behind, not wanting to leave Eliza alone. A bright flash was accompanied by a loud thunk that I felt as much as I heard. Eliza flinched, dropping the rest of the way to the ground, and Gwyn quickened her step.

I wasn't so graceful. In the space of a few heartbeats, I had snatched Gary up roughly from his fearful crouch and staggered several yards away, shouting incoherent curses like my ass was on fire. I approached Gwyn, still staggering to the point of nearly falling, and pressed Gary into her arms. I spun back toward the house, ready to drag Eliza out by her ankles, and nearly knocked her to the ground as I ran into her.

Gwyn watched the whole display impassively, even when I shoved the dog into her arms. I fussed over and apologized to Eliza, who was calm and completely fine. Neither of us were really looking, but Gwyn brought a hand up to hide her mouth as she began to laugh. I pretended not to notice.

Epilogue

We were the only survivors of a plague that… just kidding. I assumed there were other survivors, but we only ever saw signs of their passing for our first several weeks together. Whatever had turned everything upside down was still a mystery to us, but one thing was made perfectly clear as we traveled; The vast majority of people were dead or had been turned into monsters.

The radio in the ambulance worked, and we found a few stations that were broadcasting. Two of them were conspiracy theorists having meltdowns. Their channels went silent in less than a week.

One channel sounded official, but we could barely make out any of the words through the static. Eliza set to decoding the message but gave up after days of frustrating work that resulted in the words "compliance", "teen" (assumed to be the ass end of quarantine), and "help". The last word seemed to be a request and not an offer.

That was discouraging for all of us. We were being forced to accept that life had changed and that nothing would ever be the same again. Worse, we were in the dark and had no idea where to go or what to do. Our checklist had one word.

SURVIVE

The end of book one.

Make sure to check out my other books. "At Roughly, For About" is my current favorite, and I like to think you'd enjoy it, too. We have fun around here.

If you'd like to contact me, my email is Johnfjustice8@gmail.com.

www.ingramcontent.com/pod-product-compliance
Lightning Source LLC
LaVergne TN
LVHW050009170826
845677LV00023B/3398

9798846443808